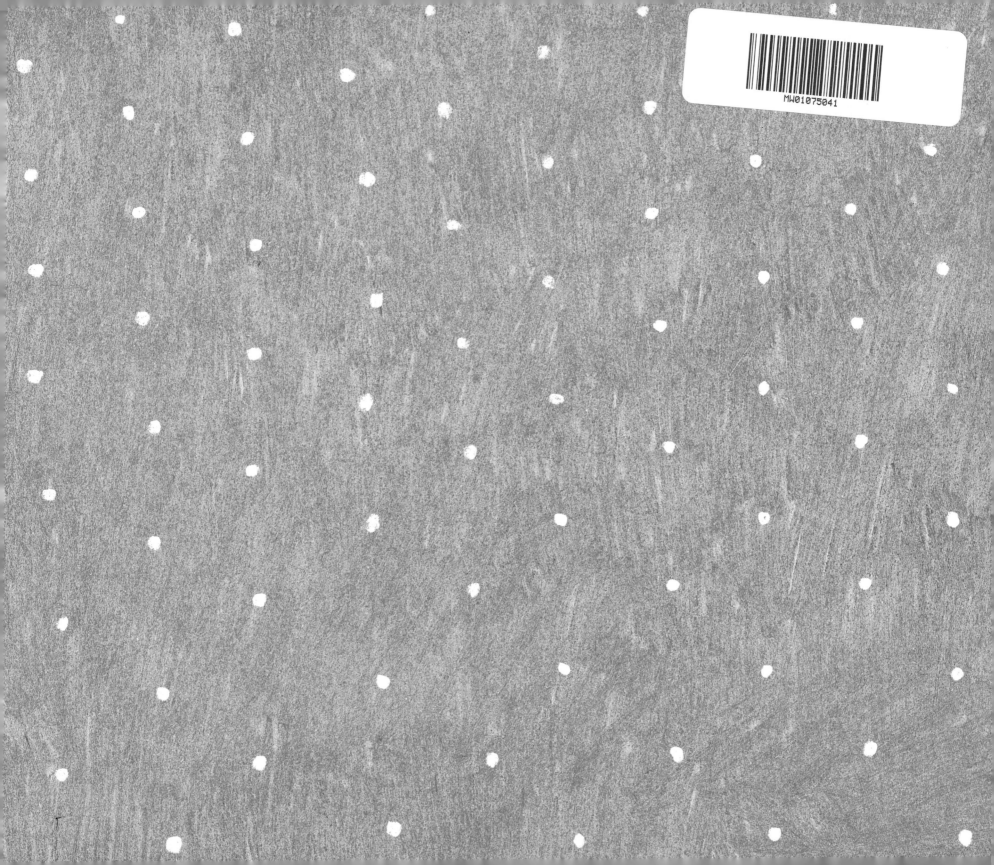

To Lizzy, a great intern,
an even better editor. –J. Y.

Library of Congress Cataloging-in-Publication Data

Names: Yolen, Jane, author. | Shleifer, Maya, illustrator.
Title: Too many golems / Jane Yolen ; [illustrated by] Maya Shleifer.
Description: San Francisco : Chronicle Books, [2024] | Audience: Ages 5-8.
Identifiers: LCCN 2023014155 | ISBN 9781797212142 (hardcover)
Subjects: LCSH: Golem--Juvenile fiction. | Jewish mythology--Juvenile
  fiction. | Hebrew language--Juvenile fiction. | Helping behavior --
  Juvenile fiction. | Humorous stories. | CYAC: Golem--Fiction.
  | Jews--Fiction. | Hebrew language--Fiction. | Helpfulness--Fiction. |
  Humorous stories. | LCGFT: Humorous fiction.
Classification: LCC PZ7.Y78 To 2024 | DDC 813.54 [E]--dc23/eng/20230411
LC record available at https://lccn.loc.gov/2023014155

Manufactured in China.

MIX
Paper | Supporting
responsible forestry
FSC™ C008047
FSC
www.fsc.org

Design by Ryan Hayes.
Typeset in Harriet Text.
The illustrations in this book were rendered in pastel pencils and wax crayons.

10 9 8 7 6 5 4 3 2 1

Chronicle books and gifts are available at special quantity discounts to corporations, professional associations, literacy programs, and other organizations. For details and discount information, please contact our premiums department at corporatesales@chroniclebooks.com or at 1-800-759-0190.

Chronicle Books LLC
680 Second Street
San Francisco, California 94107

Chronicle Books—we see things differently. Become part of our community at www.chroniclekids.com.

Too MANY GoLEMS

Jane Yolen

Maya Shleifer

chronicle books·san francisco

The rabbi's son Abi, short for Absalom, was in trouble.

Again.

He bought a bagel at the deli
and left without paying.
He was reading a comic book
at the time and just forgot.

"No bagels for a week,"
said his father.

"No allowance for a week,"
said his mother.

He said a bad word to his Hebrew teacher
because he didn't *know* it was a bad word,
only that it made the older kids
at school laugh.

When scolded, he said it again,
hoping for a better reaction.

"No comics for a week," said his father.

"Send a handwritten apology to your
teacher," said his mother.

Worst of all, he took a scroll
from the synagogue basement.

An old scroll. A frayed scroll.

A tattered and torn and worn scroll
that he thought no one would miss,
and he used it for Hebrew practice.

He stuck it on the wall of his bedroom
where he could read it secretly,
even though he didn't know
what the words meant.

The next morning,
before getting up,
he lay in his bed reading
the words to himself
to be certain he had
them right.

Then he stood, as if on the bimah,
saying the words out loud,
davening like the old men at prayers.

But he thought he could do better,
so he sang the words like a cantor,
each note a different word . . .

And at last, he said the words a fourth time,
carefully, respectfully, perfectly.
This time, he thought, dayenu.
It was enough.

But the words were not a prayer,
a poem of praise, a song of joy.

They were
a summons
to monsters.

Abi didn't know that,
but his mother's cat Kibbitz knew,
and she hid under the bed, growling.

All at once
    there came three knocks on the front door.

Not small, tentative, *I-hope-I-haven't-disturbed-you* knocks.
These were loud knocks. *Get-under-the-bed-with-the-cat!* knocks.

Kibbitz was still growling. But Abi, who had read way too many superhero comics, gathered his courage and bravely ran to open the door.

As he ran, there was a final knock. The walls trembled.

The Shabbat glasses clinked together in the sideboard.

The candlesticks clanked together on the mantelpiece.

The door yawned open.
Abi stared into the abyss.

There were ten huge clay men, gray and grizzled, some of them standing on tippy-toes, peering through the door.

He counted again and again, just to be sure. They moved as if they were human, though they definitely were not.

The largest one had a hand raised
as if to strike the door again.

He opened his toothless clay mouth and said,
"We are the Ten Golems, here to help you
sort out your misery.

We win every fight.

You called?"

Abi was confused.
Nowhere in what he'd recited
had been the word *golem*.
Besides, he knew golems weren't actually real.
They were like trolls in fairy tales, only Jewish.
And there was only one of them at a time.
Ten golems were nine golems too many.

Oh boy, was he in trouble.

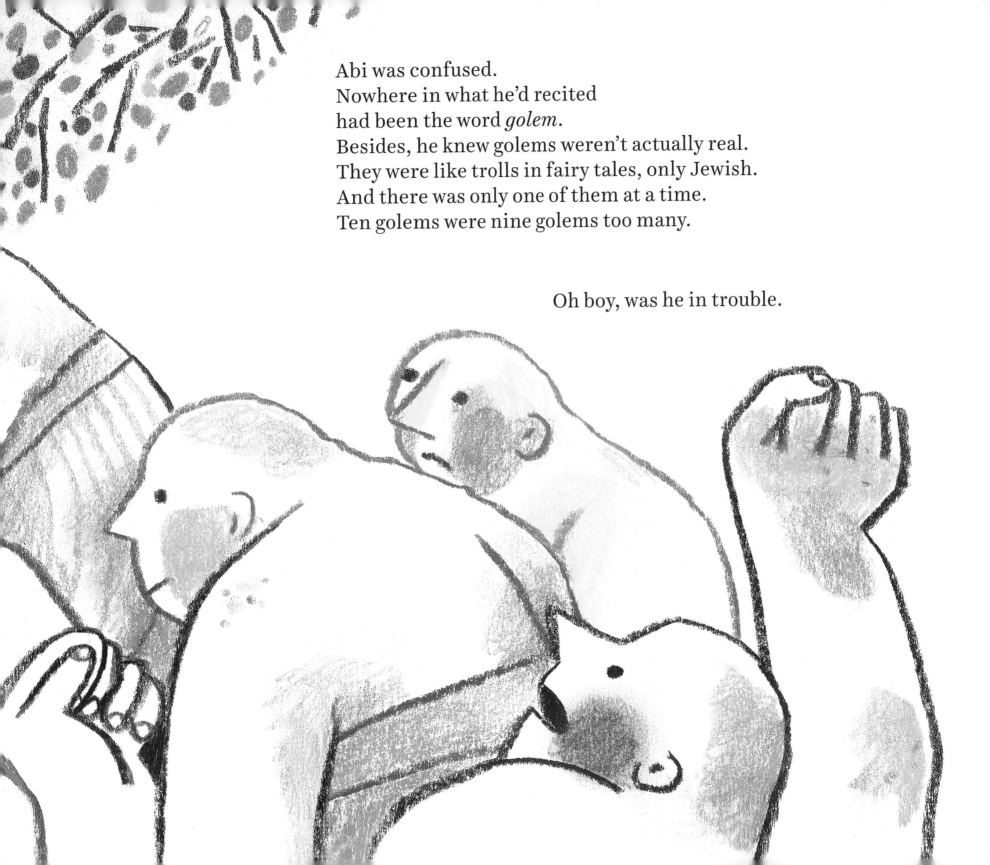

Suddenly Abi knew what to do.
His mother had taught him to be a good host.
His father had taught him to treat every stranger as a friend.

And what, Abi asked himself, *is stranger than a gang of golems?*

He opened the door wider.
"Want a cookie? A glass of milk?"

"We neither eat nor drink,"
said the biggest golem.
"We only fight."

Abi shrugged. "I can work with that."

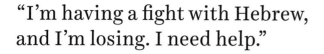

"I'm having a fight with Hebrew, and I'm losing. I need help."

"We fight your Hebrew teacher?" asked the second-largest golem, cracking his knuckles till they sounded like fireworks.

Abi shook his head.
"No, no! Just fight the language."

The smallest golem said,
"Impossible. Fight an aleph?
A bet?"

"I called for help," Abi said. "Are you saying you can't help me?"

The Ten Golems looked at one another and reached a silent agreement.

So once a week, except on the holiest of holidays,
the golems arrived together to help Abi with his Hebrew.

They never threatened him—but oh, did they yell
and shake their fists at the grammar.

At the end of each session, they taught him golem songs like
"Made from Clay!" and "Hail Prague!" and "Heave-Ho for Rabbi Loew"
or told stories about golems around the world.

Seven years later, when Abi had his bar mitzvah,
his Hebrew was perfect.

"Even better than perfect!" said the surprised rabbi.
The Ten Golems sat in the back row at shul,
singing along to the prayers in their cracked voices
and davening with the old men.

And at the party after, all ten of them danced
with the elder ladies to the tunes of a wild klezmer band.

The next day, they
were gone for good.
And Abi, now called
a young man,
considered becoming
an astronaut,
a social worker,
a prizefighter,
or a rabbi.

But not,
he thought,
a golem.

There were too many
of them already.

Rabbi Loew and His Golem

The most famous legend of the golem begins in the late 1500s, when Rabbi Judah Loew became chief rabbi of Prague. Rabbi Loew was an expert in kabbalah, a kind of religious Jewish magic.

Back then the Jewish people in Prague were being persecuted, and Rabbi Loew—so the story goes—went down to a riverbank and created a monstrous figure of a man out of riverbank clay to protect them. He animated the figure through kabbalah, by calling out God's secret name.

The monster was called the golem, and he had only one task: to save the Jewish people! He lumbered to the gates of the ghetto, where the Jewish people lived, and fought back against those who had come to do them harm. The golem had such power that the oppressors ran away, terrified, never to return.

While grateful to the golem, Rabbi Loew believed that his creation had been against God's will, because only God can create a human from dirt, mud, and clay. So the rabbi took the golem to the attic of his house, where he sat the creature down and stripped the golem of his life force.

Some people say that a mass of clay still exists in that attic to this day. But it would take another Rabbi Loew (or perhaps a child with knowledge of a certain Hebrew prayer) to reanimate the golem.

Stories of monsters can be traced back to the earliest of times and across the globe—some of the monsters good, some bad; some homegrown, some created by magicians, wizards, and gods. But the golem is the one monster specifically created to help the Jewish people. Today, with the rise in antisemitism all over the world, it would be nice if we had a golem to save us. But what we have is a story to give us courage and hope. And to remind us that those are good things to help us through difficult times.

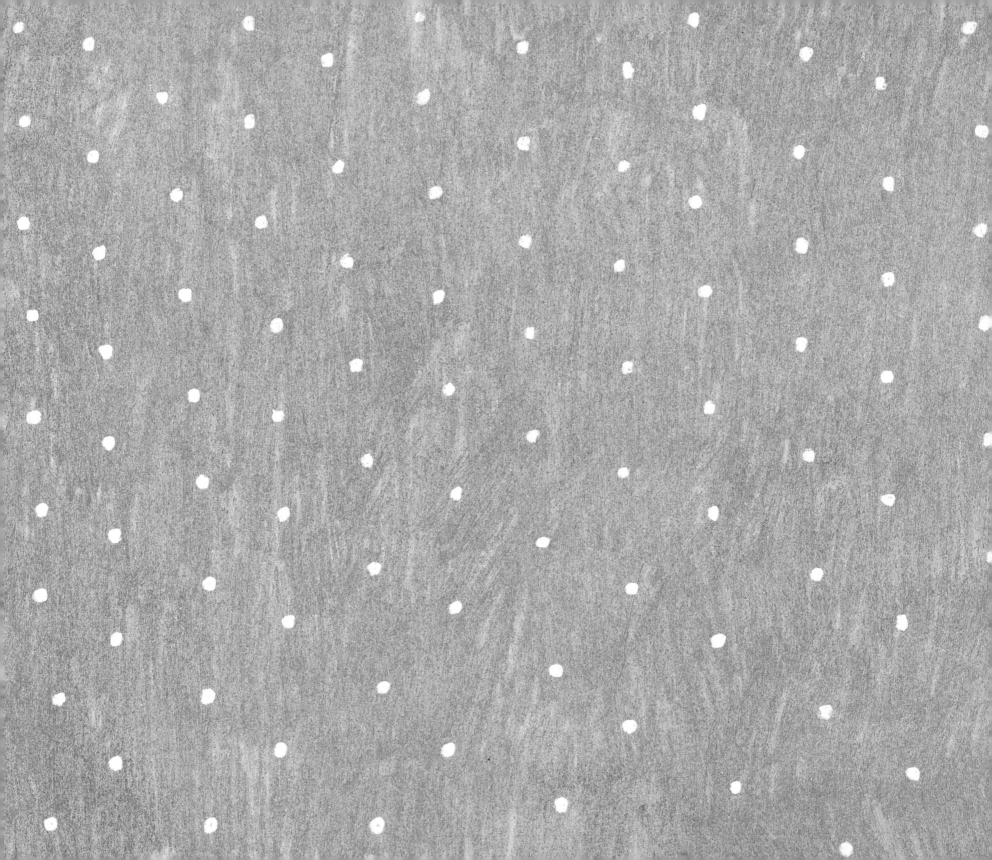